# Mermaid Janine

First published in England in 1991 by André Deutsch Children's Books, an imprint of Scholastic Children's Books, Scholastic Publications Ltd.

ISBN 0-590-46594-5

12 11 10 9 8 7 6 5 4 3 2 1        3 4 5 6 7 8/9

Printed in the U.S.A.      08

First Scholastic printing, May 1993

# Mermaid Janine

## Iolette Thomas

### Illustrated by Jennifer Northway

**SCHOLASTIC INC.**
New York  Toronto  London  Auckland  Sydney

Janine chattered happily as she walked home with her mother. "I'm glad we're nearly home," she said, as they passed a television shop, "because my favorite cartoon is on."

"And I'm glad," puffed her mother, "because these shopping bags get heavier every week."

As they opened the door, Janine saw a letter on the mat. She rushed to pick it up. "It's from your cousin Emily in Antigua," she told her mother. "Look at the stamp." "That's good," smiled her mother, putting it down on the kitchen table, "Emily owes me a letter." Janine was disappointed. "Aren't you going to read it?" she asked. "Yes, but not until I've put away the shopping," her mother replied. "I'll help," offered Janine, forgetting about her cartoon; she wanted to hear all the latest news about the family in Antigua.

By the time her mother had collected baby Ama from their next door neighbor, Maisie, Janine had put everything away. She and Ama ate cookies while their mother opened the letter. A photograph fell out.

"Who are all those people?" asked Janine, eagerly.

"That one is my cousin Emily," said her mother, pointing. "Perhaps the letter will tell us who the others are."

She read quickly, "Emily says she hopes everyone is okay, and to tell you and Ama hello. She is sorry she didn't write sooner, but she was busy organizing the Sunday School picnic, which was held last week, on the beach. The photograph is of some of the children."

Janine looked at the photograph but the only one she recognized was
Kevin, cousin Emily's son. She had seen pictures of him before.
"Did you swim when you were small?" asked Janine.
"Yes, we swam all the time," replied her mother. She put the letter down
and smiled, thinking of bygone days.
"My," said her mother, "hasn't Kevin grown since his last photograph.
Emily says he swims like a fish, and won the race for the under 8s."

Janine couldn't swim, but she wished she could — for miles and miles and miles. That night she practiced in the bath. Soon, the floor was soaking wet. Her mother was cross.

"I was only trying to swim," explained Janine.
Her mother looked thoughtful. "Perhaps it is time I taught you," she said.
"We'll go to the new Leisure Center on Friday."

When Friday came, Janine's mother took Ama to the nursery at the Leisure Center, and then she and Janine went to the changing room.

The swimming pool was crowded, and Janine decided not to get wet without her mother to hold her. But her mother had forgotten one important thing — she couldn't wear her glasses in the water and without them she could scarcely see.

"Come on now," she said, peering at the nearest child, but it wasn't Janine.

"I can't teach you without my glasses," she explained later, as they collected Ama, "but they arrange swimming lessons here, I think."

"Yes," said the receptionist, "we have a course of twelve lessons for beginners, and it starts next Friday." She added Janine's name to the list. On Friday, the swimming instructor introduced himself to the children. "My name is Rodney," he said. "Now you won't learn to swim today, but you should be able to swim the length of this pool by the end of the course, and if you do you will get a special certificate."

Janine enjoyed her first lesson, even though she got several mouthfuls of water and her eyes stung a little. By the end of the fifth lesson she could jump into the water, hold her breath and pick up a brick from the bottom of the pool, but she still couldn't swim properly.

At the end of her eighth lesson, Janine could swim the width of the pool, but she still couldn't manage a length.

"I can go a little way, and then I have to stop," she complained.
"You need extra practice," said her father, and he offered to take her early
on Sunday mornings when the pool would be half empty.

"You'll have to strengthen your legs," said Maisie, "and eat lots of vegetables, they will give you energy."
Janine hated vegetables, especially cabbage and spinach but, because she was so eager to swim her length, she ate vegetables every day and skipped rope to make her legs stronger.

By the end of her tenth lesson, she could nearly manage a length.

"Did you eat ALL of your vegetables?" asked Maisie.

"No, but I did eat some," said Janine, "I'll promise to eat all of them for the next two weeks if it will help." And she did. She had beans on Friday, peas on Saturday, sweetcorn on Sunday, cabbage on Monday, carrots on Tuesday, potatoes on Wednesday and spinach on Thursday.

On the day of her twelfth lesson, Janine changed into her bathing suit.
Her mother said, "Don't be too upset if you can't swim your length today.
I can easily put your name down for the next course of lessons." She gave
Janine a hug for good luck.

When it was Janine's turn, Rodney said, "Start when I blow the whistle.
Now, ready, set . . ." and he blew the whistle. Janine swam and swam, she
felt like a mermaid and she could hear the other children cheering.
Soon her legs began to feel tired.
"Don't stop," she told herself, "it's not far."
Then her legs felt very tired. Janine really wanted to stop, but she thought
of all the vegetables she would have to eat for the next twelve weeks, and
sprinted ahead.

At last her hand touched the end of the pool.

"Well done," said her mother, "I wasn't sure that you could make it."

"Neither was I," said Janine, and she told her mother what had kept her going.

Her mother laughed. "As you've been so good," she said, "I think you deserve a treat. What would you like?"

"Hamburger and fries, please," said Janine, and before her mother could say a word she added quickly, "with a salad, of course."